◆ ◆ ◆ ◆ CHARLOTTE HERMAN

Max Malone and the Great Cereal Rip-off

◆ Illustrated by
CATHERINE SMITH

A Redfeather Book

Henry Holt and Company ◆ New York

For my sweet Heshy, with love. —C.H.

Published by Henry Holt and Company, Inc.,
115 West 18th Street, New York, New York 10011.
Published in Canada by Fitzhenry & Whiteside Limited,
195 Allstate Parkway, Markham, Ontario L3R 4T8.

Library of Congress Cataloging-in-Publication Data
Herman, Charlotte.
  Max Malone and the great cereal rip-off / Charlotte Herman ;
illustrated by Catherine Smith.
  (Redfeather books)
  Summary: Tired of being cheated by the cereal companies, Max
decides to fight back after not receiving a free glow-in-the-dark
sticker in his box of Choco-Fish.
  ISBN 0-8050-1069-6
  [1. Cereals, Prepared—Fiction. 2. Toys—Fiction.] Smith,
Cat Bowman, ill. II. Title. III. Series.
PZ7.H4313Max   1990
[E]—dc20   89-26920

Henry Holt books are available at special discounts
for bulk purchases for sales promotions, premiums,
fund-raising, or educational use. Special editions
or book excerpts can also be created to specification.

    For details contact:

    Special Sales Director
    Henry Holt and Company, Inc.
    115 West 18th Street
    New York, New York 10011

First Edition
Designed by Victoria Hartman
Printed in the United States of America
10 9 8 7 6 5 4 3 2 1

Contents

Waiting for Motor Man

Max Malone sat on his front steps. He was waiting for the mailman. He had been looking forward to the mail every day for a month. But it seemed like a year. It always took forever to get the things he sent away for. And Max was forever sending away for things: stickers, personalized pencils, photo mugs, and creepy crawlers.

This time Max had sent away for something special: a robot. It was called Motor Man. Max had had to send in two dollars and two proofs of purchase from Crummies breakfast cereal to get

Motor Man. The two dollars was all he had left of his life savings. And before he could send away the proofs of purchase, he had had to finish the cereal. His mother had a rule about cereal: "We buy it, you eat it."

So Max had to eat his way through two boxes of Crummies. His sister, Rosalie, had helped him. Rosalie loved sweet cereal. The sweeter the better. Sometimes she even sprinkled sugar on the cereal. Still, there was a lot left for Max. The cereal in the first box had tasted pretty good. By the time he'd finished the cereal in the second box, he felt sick. But Motor Man was worth it. He was the color of silver and three inches tall, and didn't need any batteries. All you had to do was wind him up. And now that summer vacation had begun, Max would have lots of time to play with him.

Where was that mailman? Max was getting impatient. To help pass the time, he sorted through his collection of baseball cards that he kept in an album. Max loved to collect baseball cards. Once he'd even thought about becoming a baseball player. His favorite card right now was the Kirby Puckett he got in a trade with Austin Healy for an unknown player of the 1970s.

Austin was only six years old and didn't seem to mind that his parents had named him after a car. "My father always wanted an Austin Healy," Austin had told Max when they first met. "It was his favorite car. But he couldn't afford one. Then I came along. So now I'm his Austin Healy."

Austin didn't know anything about collecting baseball cards either. He had just received his cousin's old collection, and one card was just as good as another. While Max was admiring Kirby Puckett, he heard a voice.

"Hey, Max. Watcha doin'?"

Max looked up to see Austin waving to him from across the street.

"Waiting for the mailman," Max called back. "And looking through my baseball cards."

"My cousin gave me some new ones. Wanna see them?"

"Sure. Come on over."

Austin was the youngest kid on the block and the newest kid in the neighborhood. He loved to hang around Max, who was nine and the oldest kid on the block. At first Max wasn't sure how he felt about having a little kid hanging around. But now that Austin had baseball cards to trade, it was a different story. Austin climbed up the steps and sat down next to Max.

"Tell me which cards you think are good," said Austin, handing him the pile.

Max flipped through the cards, hoping to spot a valuable one. A Mickey Mantle. Or a Hank Aaron. He was so busy with the cards, he almost forgot about the mailman. And Motor Man. Finally his eyes fell upon an Andre Dawson card. It was one he had wanted for a long time. Max was so excited, he almost fell off the steps. But he had to control himself. He pointed to the picture of Andre Dawson.

"This one's okay," Max told Austin. "I'll swap you for it."

Austin leaned over to look at the card. "Andre Dawson, huh? My cousin said this card is a good one."

"It sure is," said Max. "And that's why I'll give you two of mine. Two for one." Max picked out two cards he didn't care about. They weren't worth much either. He handed them to Austin. Ah, another easy trade. Max Malone strikes again. And he'd better keep striking fast. Before Austin learned about baseball cards.

"Two for one and they're in mint condition," said Max. He showed Austin the Andre Dawson card. "If you look very closely, you can see that it has a slight bend in the corner. But I'll swap you anyway, Austin. You're a great kid."

"Gee, thanks, Max. You sure do know a lot about baseball cards." He gathered all his old cards together. And his two newest ones. Then he ran off.

Max carefully placed his Dawson card next to the one of Kirby Puckett. He thought about how lucky he was to have a little kid like Austin Healy living right across the street. He was still thinking about that when Ray the mailman came walking up the steps. By this time Max had forgotten all about Ray.

"Hi, there, Max. I've got something for you. I think this is what you've been waiting for."

As soon as Max spotted the brown box, he knew just what it was.

"Wow!" he said as he took the box and ran into his house. "Andre Dawson and Motor Man. Is this my lucky day or what?"

Rip-off

Max ripped open the package. He pulled Motor Man out of the box. Motor Man was three inches tall and the color of silver. "See, just like the picture," he said.

"It will be a piece of junk," said Rosalie.

Rosalie was two years older than Max and thought she knew everything. Sometimes it seemed as if she really did. Once when Max ordered greeting cards to sell for fabulous prizes, Rosalie had told him that nobody would buy any. She was right. The cards were ugly and had long, corny poems written inside. Max was sure that if a sick person received one of those get-well cards, he or she would feel even sicker.

And then there was the time Max's scout troop had to sell chocolate candy bars to raise money for a trip to the Wisconsin Dells. Rosalie predicted that Max would eat the candy before he had a chance to sell any. She was right again—even though she had helped him eat almost half of it.

But this time Rosalie was wrong. Motor Man was not a piece of junk.

Max wound up the robot and set him on the kitchen floor. Motor Man ran around in a circle. He could run in circles or straight, depending on which way you turned his feet. Max had him running in all directions. "Wow, this is great," he said. "I should've bought two of them. Then they could race each other." He wound up Motor Man again, and the robot scooted under the dining-room table.

"See, it's not a piece of junk," he told Rosalie.

"Give it time," said Rosalie. "Sooner or later it'll fall on its face."

Max tried to ignore her. She just didn't want to admit she was wrong.

"Hey, I know," said Max as he placed Motor Man on his hand and watched him run up and down his arm. "If Gordy got his Motor Man today, we could have them compete." Gordy was Max's friend. He liked to send away for things too. In fact, Gordy was the one who had told Max about Motor Man. They had sent away at the same time.

"Sure you could compete," said Rosalie. "You could compete to see which one falls on its face first." She took Motor Man away from Max and examined him. "Just as I thought. It's not built to last. It'll fall apart before the day's over."

Max grabbed Motor Man back from Rosalie. He would show her. He wound him up again. He showed her how Motor Man walked from hand to hand. And how he climbed a ramp made from a book. And how he ran around in a circle and fell on his face.

When Max picked him up, he saw that Motor Man wasn't working anymore. He tried to wind him up. He wouldn't wind. He shook him. Nothing. He threw Motor Man on the floor. Motor Man gave one last sputter and then just lay there. Rosalie gave him an "I told you so" look.

"It's a piece of junk," said Max. "I was ripped off."

"I told you so," said Rosalie. "It happens all the time."

Max sat on the floor, frowning. He wasn't sure what bothered him more—a broken Motor Man or a right Rosalie. "What happens all the time?"

"They fool you all the time. First it's TV. Then it's cereal. Like Super Sam. On TV he was a hero. He climbed mountains, he hunted lions in Africa. And he went deep-sea diving. So you bought him—"

"And he didn't do anything," Max finished for her.

"Yes," said Rosalie. "Then his head fell off. You've got to stop believing all those ads and commercials. There are always people out there who make it a business of gypping other people. You can't trust them. They just want your money."

Max didn't want to hang around the house listening to Rosalie remind him of how often he had been gypped. He threw Motor Man in the garbage and went off to the playground, kicking a pebble along the way. It wasn't fair. He had waited a whole month for that robot, and it didn't even work.

At the park Max saw Gordy. He ran over to tell him about Motor Man.

"It was a rip-off," he said.

"I know," said Gordy. "Mine was too."

They climbed the monkey bars and sat there, talking about how they were cheated.

"People who cheat other people should go to jail," said Gordy.

"Yeah," Max agreed. He thought about the Crummies cereal company. "They shouldn't be allowed to gyp kids."

Gordy jumped off the monkey bars. "But I just sent away for something really good this time. Muscle Man. You get him from Scary Berries. Just two dollars and ninety-five cents and three proofs of purchase. My father said it looks like a quality item. The best part is that Muscle Man comes in lots of little pieces. And when you put him together, you learn all about the human body."

Max was interested in the human body, all right. And it would be fun to put Muscle Man together. Even if he had to eat three boxes of Scary Berries, it wouldn't be so bad. As long as he had Rosalie to help him. And he didn't think it would be too hard to convince his mother to give him the two dollars and ninety-five cents. He hadn't asked her for any extra spending money in a long time.

The thought of getting Muscle Man almost made Max forget about Motor Man. Motor Man was a piece of junk. But Muscle Man would be different. It was a quality item. He couldn't wait!

Scary Berries

The next morning when Mrs. Malone was getting ready to go to the supermarket, Max told her, "I'd better go with you. I can help you carry the packages."

"That's thoughtful of you, Max. Thank you." And as they were leaving the house, she added, "Which cereal do you want this time?"

"Scary Berries," Max answered. It was weird the way his mother could read his mind.

"And what are they offering?"

"Muscle Man. You put him together and learn

all about the human body. It's very educational."
Max thought it might be a good idea to throw in
that last remark. His mother believed in anything
educational—museums, encyclopedias, trips to
Washington, D.C.

As they were getting into the car, Austin called
out to Max from across the street, where he was
tossing a ball in the air. "Thanks a million for the
great baseball cards, Max."

"He certainly does look up to you," said Mrs.
Malone.

"What does he know," said Max as he ducked
into the car. "He's just a little kid." As Mrs. Malone
drove off, Max glanced at Austin in the rearview
mirror. He thought about their trade. Austin was
happy with the cards Max had given him. And
besides, nobody forced him to trade.

At the supermarket Max waited patiently while
his mother browsed through the Bibb lettuce and
checked the farm-fresh eggs. She loaded the
wagon with lots of boring stuff like coffee,

eggplant, and celery. When they finally reached the aisle where the cereal was displayed, Max spotted the Scary Berries right away. The box was purple and showed an almost naked man with muscles.

HEY, KIDS!
HAVE FUN WHILE YOU LEARN
SEND FOR MUSCLE MAN
ONLY $2.95
AND 3 PROOFS OF PURCHASE
NOT AVAILABLE AT ANY STORE

Max pointed out Muscle Man to his mother. "Look, Mom. Just three boxes and two ninety-five. It's a real bargain for a quality item like that."

"It seems to me that two dollars and ninety-five cents is a lot of money for something like that," said his mother.

"I can always use some of my birthday money that you put away."

"I'm saving it," said Mrs. Malone. "For college."

"Come on, Mom," said Max. "I'm only in the fourth grade. Can't I just have two ninety-five?" Max waited nervously while his mother was making up her mind.

"Well, I suppose so. After all, it's for something educational—I think. But you'll have to eat all three boxes."

"I will," said Max. "And Rosalie will help me."

Max picked out three of the small-size boxes. He didn't want to eat more Scary Berries than he had to. His mother chose some Nature Blend for herself. "It's high in fiber and protein, and low in sugar," she told Max. Then she began to read the ingredients out loud: " 'Whole-grain wheat, barley, oats, corn, rice, figs, dates, apples, raisins, peaches, and coconut.' This is what you and Rosalie should be eating."

"What are they offering?" asked Max.

"Free yogurt," Mrs. Malone answered.

"No thanks," said Max.

As soon as they got home, Max took out two bowls, two spoons, and a carton of low-fat milk.

When Rosalie came into the kitchen, she saw the cereal and said, "Oh, yummy. Scary Berries." She sat down at the table. "I can't believe you're going to send away for this Muscle Man thing. You never learn your lesson." She watched as Max poured the little grape ghosts into the bowls.

"You should have bought the giant economy size," she said. "It's a better buy. Of course they won't advertise it so you can see it. They print the price per ounce so tiny you can hardly read it."

Max tried not to pay attention to Rosalie. He wasn't going to let her be a spoilsport. Anyway, the sooner he finished the cereal, the sooner he could send away for Muscle Man.

Who knows? Max thought. Maybe someday I'll be a doctor.

Purple Teeth

Scary Berries were purple. And when Max poured milk on them, the milk turned purple too. Max had never eaten Scary Berries before. He didn't like the way they tasted. He thought they were too sweet. Rosalie didn't think they were sweet enough. She looked at her mother. Her mother wasn't looking at her. Mrs. Malone was busy looking at her new orders for memo pads. She sold personalized memo pads through the mail.

Rosalie put her fingers in the sugar bowl and sprinkled sugar all over her Scary Berries.

"Ugh," said Max. "How can you do that? Your teeth will fall out."

Mrs. Malone didn't like it when Rosalie added sugar to cereal. Especially to cereal that was already sweetened. In fact, she didn't really approve of sugared cereal. But whenever she bought more nutritional cereal like Fiber Flakes or Bran Bits, Max and Rosalie never touched it. Mrs. Malone also felt that Max and Rosalie would eventually get sick of all that sweet cereal and give it up. So far that hadn't happened. How could Rosalie give up all that sweet and sometimes colorful cereal? And how could Max give up all those great things to send away for? The only thing Fiber Flakes ever offered was panty hose.

While he was eating, Max studied the box of cereal. "Artificial grape flavor. . . . Offer good while supply lasts. . . . Allow 4–6 weeks for delivery."

Four to six weeks. Another long wait. School might be starting by then. Max wondered if they would be learning about the human body in the fourth grade.

By the next day Max and Rosalie had finished the first box of Scary Berries. But Max had a hard time getting through the second box. He didn't think he could eat any more of them.

"I don't think I can eat any more of this," he told Rosalie.

"I can eat yours for you," offered Rosalie as she sprinkled sugar on her cereal.

Max thought this might be a good idea. He could get whatever cereal he wanted, and Rosalie would eat it all up. But when he imagined Rosalie eating all that sweet cereal, he saw her getting fatter and fatter and all her teeth falling out. Rosalie was bossy and a know-it-all. But she was still his sister. He couldn't let that happen to her.

By the end of the week, Max and Rosalie had finished two boxes of Scary Berries. They had just one more box to go. Max was determined to finish it. He really wanted Muscle Man. He needed him.

But no matter how hard he tried, he just couldn't eat any more of it. Scary Berries made him feel sick. They made his teeth purple.

Max took his bowl of cereal and went into the bathroom. When he thought nobody was looking, he flushed the cereal down the toilet.

"Aha!" said Rosalie, who came up from behind.

"Promise you won't tell," said Max.

"What if I do tell?"

"Then I'll tell about the sugar," Max answered.

"I promise," said Rosalie.

Max made a promise too. He felt bad about wasting food. "I won't throw any more cereal down the toilet. I'll eat the Scary Berries. Even if I do get sick. Even if I do get purple teeth."

After all, there was no other choice. Or was there?

Austin to the Rescue

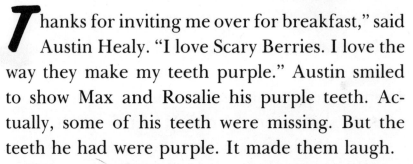

*T*hanks for inviting me over for breakfast," said Austin Healy. "I love Scary Berries. I love the way they make my teeth purple." Austin smiled to show Max and Rosalie his purple teeth. Actually, some of his teeth were missing. But the teeth he had were purple. It made them laugh.

"My mom doesn't buy me sweet cereal too often," said Austin. "Maybe about two times a year. Mostly she buys Fiber Flakes and Bran Bits." All three of them made faces and gagging sounds.

Rosalie and Austin finished the Scary Berries

from the third box, and Max got ready to send for Muscle Man. He cut out the mail-in certificate from the box and read it over carefully before he filled it out.

Please send $\_1\_$ Muscle Man (Men).
For each Muscle Man, I have enclosed
$2.95 and 3 proofs of purchase from
any size Scary Berries.
Check or money order only.

He clearly printed his name and address, and included his complete zip code to ensure delivery. Then his mother wrote him a check for two dollars and ninety-five cents. He placed the certificate and check in an envelope, addressed the envelope, and put a stamp on it.

"Since you helped me eat the cereal, you can help me mail away for Muscle Man," Max said to Austin as they left the house.

"Muscle Man will be a piece of junk," Rosalie called out after them.

Max and Austin walked to the corner, where Max dropped the envelope in the mailbox.

"Can I help you play with Muscle Man when it comes?" Austin asked.

"Sure," said Max. "I'll teach you all about the human body."

On the way back home Max asked, "Did you get any more baseball cards?"

"No," Austin answered. "But Mrs. Filbert told me that she's having a garage sale at the end of summer, and she might have some cards to sell."

Mrs. Filbert lived on their block and loved to have garage sales. Years ago, when Max first heard about Mrs. Filbert's garage sale, he thought it meant that she was selling her garage. But he found out that she was just selling unwanted things that were in her garage or in her house.

Mrs. Filbert's children were all grown and lived away from home. Max figured that they must have collected baseball cards while they were growing up. By now the cards could be very valuable.

"Maybe I'll see you there," he told Austin.

They were almost at Max's house when Austin said, "Hey, Max, I've got a riddle for you. What has four wheels and flies?"

"A garbage truck," said Max. That was probably one of the easiest riddles around. It would take a little kid like Austin to ask something like that.

"Oh, you heard that one," said Austin, and Max could see the disappointment in his face.

"Ask me another one," said Max.

"Okay. What's black and white and red all over?"

Max knew that one too. A newspaper. But he pretended to be thinking a few seconds before he said, "I don't know. What?"

"A newspaper," said Austin, and started to laugh hysterically. "Isn't that great? And here's another one. What will keep you from going bald?"

Max hadn't heard that one before. He tried to figure out the answer, but he couldn't. "I give up," he said finally. "What will keep you from going bald?"

"Hair," said Austin. And he was practically rolling on the sidewalk. Max was laughing with him. He liked that riddle, all right. He would have to remember to try it on Rosalie and Gordy.

"Okay, Austin. Now I've got one for you. What do you call a worried grape?"

"I give up," said Austin. "What?"

"A raisin," Max answered.

"A raisin?" Austin looked puzzled. Then a grin broke out on his face. "Oh, a raisin. I get it. Because of the wrinkles. Boy, that's a good one." He gave Max a slap on the back. "Thanks for telling it to me. I'm gonna go try it on my mom. See ya." He gave Max a little wave and ran across the street.

Max watched to make certain that Austin crossed safely before turning to walk up the steps to his own house.

Free Inside

"Look," Max said to Gordy. "I never saw this cereal before. All Stars. It must be new."

Max and Gordy were browsing through the cereal section of the supermarket one day. All around them were cereal boxes of every size and color. Dentist-office music was playing.

Max and Gordy knew they would have to wait a long time for Muscle Man. So they decided that the next cereal premium they would get would be something that came right inside the box. Not something they would have to send away for.

Their mothers had given each of them money to buy one box of any kind of cereal they wanted.

But how could they decide what to get? There were so many brands of cereal, and each one was offering something special.

"It's got real strawberry flavor," Max went on, "and a superball comes inside. Or you can get a mini Frisbee in a box of Frost Bites."

"I have superballs and Frisbees all over my house," said Gordy. "How about this?" He pointed to a box of Rice Crunch. "You get a real telescope inside.".

"I once got that. It's not real. It's made mostly of cardboard, and when you look through the lens, you get dizzy."

All the cereal boxes seemed to be begging to be bought—to be calling out to Max and Gordy: FREE INSIDE! COLLECT THEM ALL! HOURS OF ENTERTAINMENT!

They saw offers for T-shirts, magic tricks, and secret decoders. Finally, Max spotted Choco-Fish.

FREE PLANETS OF THE UNIVERSE! GLOW IN THE DARK! ONE STICKER IN EACH BOX. COLLECT ALL 9!

And there on both sides of the box were the nine planets moving through space: Mercury, Venus, Earth, Mars, Jupiter, Saturn (there were rings around it!), Uranus, Neptune, and Pluto. They were large and colorful. They were beautiful.

"This is it," said Max. "This is what I'll get." Max didn't like Choco-Fish too much—all those little chocolate fish floating around and dissolving in the milk. But he loved the planets.

"I think I'll get this too," said Gordy. "The planets look like a quality item, and you can learn about astronomy."

Max was interested in astronomy. Maybe one day he'd even be an astronomer.

After serious thought as to which of the boxes of Choco-Fish to choose, Max and Gordy each picked a favorite and went up to the express lane to pay for it.

When Max returned home, his mother was in the kitchen reading a letter aloud to Rosalie. It was from a mail-order customer who had become friends with Mrs. Malone because she was always ordering memo pads. Max came in as she was finishing, "With warmest regards, Sylvia."

Max had never met Sylvia, so he didn't care about her letter. He looked through the mail, hoping to find Muscle Man. He knew it wouldn't be there yet. It had been just over a week since he sent away for it. But he was hoping. All he found were more orders for memo pads.

But today Max didn't care. He had his box of Choco-Fish and a glow-in-the-dark planet of the universe. He couldn't wait to see which one of the planets was inside. He hoped it was Saturn. He really liked those rings.

Was It a Mistake or Did You Do It on Purpose?

But you don't like Choco-Fish," Mrs. Malone reminded Max. "You don't like the way those chocolate fish float around and dissolve in the milk."

"I know," said Max as he stuck his hand inside the box, searching for the sticker. "But I do like planets that glow. I can collect all nine of them and learn about the universe."

Max couldn't find the sticker right away, so he pulled his hand out of the box. It was all sticky. He filled up two bowls with Choco-Fish. One for himself and one for Rosalie, who was sitting at the table, waiting. He still could not see the planet.

While Max was pouring the rest of the cereal into a large mixing bowl, Rosalie poured milk on her Choco-Fish and sneaked some sugar to sprinkle on top.

"It's probably not even there," she said.

"It's probably at the very bottom," Max said as he emptied out the box. He searched through the bowl of cereal. There was nothing but cereal.

Max slid quietly into his chair. "It's missing," he said, almost to himself, so Rosalie couldn't hear. "My planet is missing." It wasn't fair. He wasn't asking for the whole universe. Just one stupid planet.

"I can't believe it," he said, his voice growing louder now. "There's nothing in here. This is a real rip-off."

"I told you so," said Rosalie, and she bit a fish's head off.

Max thought about all those cereal boxes in the

supermarket. All those offers to choose from. He pounded the table with his fist. "Of all the boxes on the shelf, I had to pick this one." He poured some milk on the cereal and began eating. Choco-Fish tasted awful. And it wasn't fair that he had to eat it. He was eating it for nothing.

While Max was gagging on the Choco-Fish, he thought about all the times he was gypped. "I was ripped off lots of times," he said. "I once sent away for a top that didn't spin. My anthills had no ants, and my flower seeds came up carrots. I'm tired of it."

The phone rang and Max went to answer it. Anything to keep from eating those fish.

"Hello," he said into the phone.

"Hi. Which planet did you get?"

"I didn't get anything. Just this lousy cereal."

"I got Saturn. The one with all those rings. It really glows in the dark."

"Yeah, that's great. I'll talk to you later." He hung up the phone and sat down with a thud.

"Real great. *Gordy* gets Saturn. It's not fair. I want my planet."

"Then do something about it," said Rosalie as she bit off the fins of another fish. The milk was turning brown, and the chocolate fish were disintegrating. Max was feeling sick.

"Do what?" asked Max.

"Write a letter to the cereal company. Tell them you don't like to be ripped off."

"Maybe it was a mistake," said Max.

"Sometimes I think you're just a dumb little kid. They did it on purpose. Write the letter."

"And sometimes I think you're the bossiest sister in the universe." Then he took a pen, and a sheet from his personalized memo pad that said *From the desk of MAX MALONE*, and he wrote the letter.

Dear Choco - Fish,

There was no planet in

my box of Choco - Fish. I
don't like to be ripped
off. Was it a mistake or
did you do it on purpose ?

With warmest regards,

Max Malone

Max walked to the corner to mail the letter. On the way back he saw Austin batting a ball in front of his house. He looked so happy, playing by himself, without a worry in the world. Max decided to go across the street and pitch the ball to Austin.

Maybe he could pretend he was six years old too.

Muscle Man

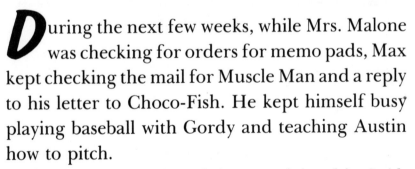

During the next few weeks, while Mrs. Malone was checking for orders for memo pads, Max kept checking the mail for Muscle Man and a reply to his letter to Choco-Fish. He kept himself busy playing baseball with Gordy and teaching Austin how to pitch.

He also spent a lot of time studying his *Guide to Baseball Cards* so he would know which cards to look for at Mrs. Filbert's garage sale. He could just imagine himself in the garage, checking out the small box of baseball cards hidden away in some dark corner. And only he, Max Malone, would be able to identify the treasures that waited for him in that box.

While other people were getting all excited at their great buys on lawn chairs and garden tools, Max would be discovering a 1952 Mickey Mantle or a 1934 Lou Gehrig. Austin would be there too, of course, but he wouldn't know the difference between one player and another.

One morning while Max was making up a list of his twenty-five most-wanted baseball cards, he heard Ray the mailman walking up the steps. He ran out to meet him.

"Another package for you, Max." Ray handed him the box.

"Thanks, Ray," said Max. He ran into the house and tore open the box. And there, in what seemed like a hundred pieces, was Muscle Man. Max spread out all the pieces on the floor—like a puzzle—and spent most of the day trying to put Muscle Man together. But the easy-to-follow directions

weren't easy to follow. Finally Max gave up and had to ask Rosalie for help.

"Can you help me put Muscle Man together?"

"It looks impossible," said Rosalie. "But I'll try."

Rosalie gave up after five minutes. "This is impossible. Even a doctor couldn't put him together."

Max collected all the pieces, put them back in the box, and went over to Gordy's house. Gordy was sitting on his front lawn, studying an anthill with his magnifying glass.

"Hey, Gordy. I got Muscle Man today and I can't put him together. Do you think you can help me?"

Gordy put down his magnifying glass. "Are you kidding? I tried to put mine together last night, but I couldn't. Even my father tried. He couldn't either. And he's a doctor."

"That's it! I've had it!" Max threw the box filled with Muscle Man pieces on the ground. "I'm tired of being ripped off. Rosalie is right. You can't trust them. They just want your money. Well, I won't be fooled, ever again!" He picked up his box and stomped off.

The next morning when Max woke up, Rosalie told him, "If you must send away for something, I know what you can send for next. You can get this cute little Moon Walker from Weird-O's. Just fifty cents and one proof of purchase. I love Weird-O's."

"No!" cried Max. "No Weird-O's, no Choco-Fish, no Scary Berries, no Crummies. No Muscle Man, no Motor Man, no cute little Moon Walker. Nothing—ever again—as long as I live."

That morning Max ate scrambled eggs for breakfast. He noticed that his mother was smiling as she made them. Max liked the way the eggs slid down his throat. Rosalie ate toast. She sprinkled sugar on it.

Max ate many different kinds of breakfasts in the days that followed. His mother was very happy to make whatever he wanted: pancakes, waffles, French toast, and cheese omelettes.

It had been a long time since breakfast tasted so good.

The Garage Sale

Summer was coming to an end. Mrs. Filbert put out signs all around the neighborhood, announcing her garage sale on the second Saturday in August.

Max woke up early that Saturday. He wanted to be the first person at the sale. He had to make sure no one got to the cards before he did.

His mother gave Max three dollars to spend because he was saving her so much money by not sending away for things. "Just don't bring back anything live. Or dead," she warned.

Max was reminded of the last time he had gone to one of Mrs. Filbert's garage sales. He had come home with a stuffed squirrel. It cost just twenty-five cents and was in mint condition. He thought he'd buy it to scare Rosalie. But the only people he had scared were his mother and himself. The squirrel was fun to look at in the daytime. But spooky at night. Max couldn't stand having it in his room. He ended up giving it to Gordy.

Max picked up his price guide and the list of his twenty-five most-wanted cards, and was off.

Mrs. Filbert and her husband lived in a large white house down the block and around the corner. The house was too large for just two people, she'd once told Mrs. Malone. And it was filled with too many things. That's why she was having so many garage sales. Max often wondered how Mrs. Filbert could have so much to sell at all those sales. Pretty soon there would be nothing left to sell, and Mr. and Mrs. Filbert would be living in an empty house.

Max turned the corner, hoping that he would be the first one there. But what he saw shocked him. There were people all over the place, walking around with lamps and picture frames. There were tables set up on the front lawn and people searching through the merchandise. One of those people was Austin Healy.

Max hurried over to where Austin was standing. He could see him looking through a box of baseball cards. This was all wrong. The box was right there on an outside table. Not hidden away in a dark corner of the garage, like it was supposed to be. And Austin—not Max—was looking through the cards.

Max poked Austin on the shoulder. "Finding anything good?"

Austin turned around. "Oh, hi, Max. They're five cents apiece. I've got fifty cents, so that means I can buy . . . ten of them." He handed Max a pile of ten cards. "Did I pick good ones?"

Max looked through the cards one at a time.

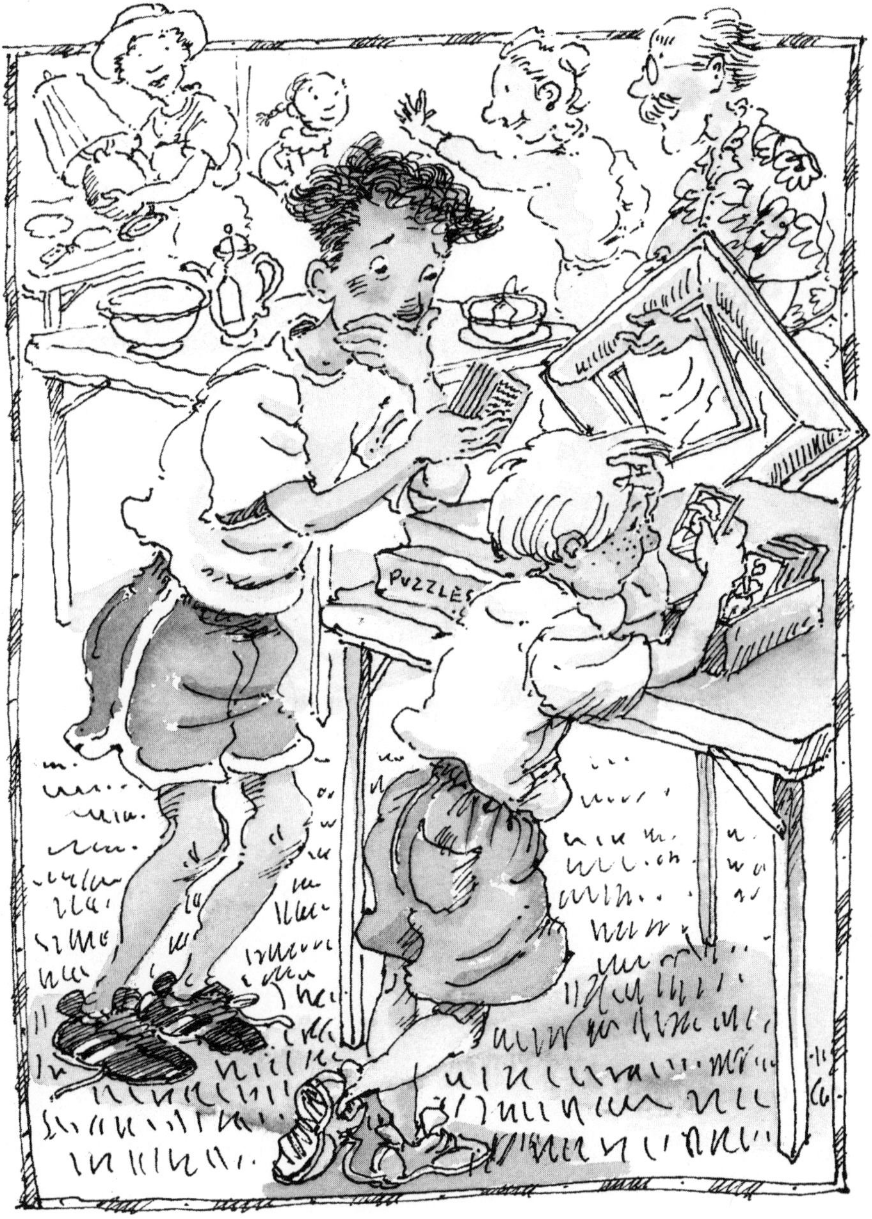
PUZZLES

Most of what he saw was nothing special. They were worth five cents, though. Some might have been worth twenty-five or even fifty cents. But there were no great finds, no star players. Until the last card. Max couldn't believe his eyes. Johnny Bench. A 1969 Johnny Bench. And it was in near-mint condition. It was a great card. He had never seen it before, except in a magazine. And he remembered reading that it was worth a lot of money. How did Austin know to pick it?

"Well, what do you think?" Austin asked.

Max started to sweat. He wanted this card for himself.

"I'm not sure. Let me see what else there is." Max searched through the box. There was nothing that he wanted. Nobody from his twenty-five most-wanted list. There was just that Johnny Bench card. And Austin had found it first. Max had to have it.

Austin didn't need it. He was just a little kid who didn't know the difference between one card and another. Max took the Johnny Bench card out of the pile to save for himself. He handed the rest of the cards to Austin.

"These are the cards you should buy," said Max. "But I don't think you should buy this other one because . . ."

Austin looked up at him, waiting for an answer. Max had a hard time looking into Austin's eyes. Little Austin Healy, who was named after a car. Who ate Scary Berries and got purple teeth. Max thought about Muscle Man and Motor Man and no planets in his Choco-Fish. He thought about the Dawson trade, and Kirby Puckett.

". . . Because I'm going to buy it for you," Max continued. "It's a great card. In fact, I'm buying you all ten of them. And they're worth a lot more than fifty cents."

"Wow! Thanks, Max. You can come over and look at them whenever you want to."

"Don't go trading your Johnny Bench card or anything. Bench played for the Reds and was one of the greatest catchers of all time. Make sure you see me first. You don't want to get ripped off." Somebody had to protect that little kid.

Max paid for the cards, and Austin ran home to show them to his mother and father. Max still had two dollars and fifty cents left. He went off to find something else to buy. Maybe something for his mother, or for Rosalie. Whatever.

Just so it wasn't dead or alive.

The Letter

Max came back from the garage sale with a pair of earrings for his mother. They looked like genuine pearls. For Rosalie he bought a copy of *Gone with the Wind*. But Max didn't even get a chance to show them what he'd bought. As soon as he got home, Rosalie opened the door and pulled him inside.

"Surprise! Close your eyes and count to one hundred."

"Why?" asked Max.

"Just do it."

Max closed his eyes and counted by tens.

"Don't cheat," said Rosalie.

Max counted by twos, then opened his eyes. "What's the surprise?"

Rosalie handed him an envelope. It was addressed to Max Malone, and it was open.

"Hey, you opened my mail," said Max.

"It fell open. Now look inside."

For the second time that day Max couldn't believe what he saw. "Wow! My planets! All nine of them!"

There was a letter, too:

Max Malone
18 Forest Ave.
Evanston, IL 60202

Dear Max,

We are very sorry that there was no planet in your box of Choco-Fish. It was a mistake. Sometimes the machines get stuck. So here are nine

free planets of the universe. They glow in the dark.

Thank you for eating Choco-Fish.

Sincerely,

Wendy Wheatfield

Wendy Wheatfield
Consumer Relations Dept.
Choco-Fish, Inc.

"It was a mistake!" Max shouted. "I knew all the time it wasn't a gyp." He spilled out the stickers onto the kitchen table. They were large and colorful, just like the pictures on the box. There was Mars and Venus and Earth and Saturn with its rings. All nine of them were there. On the back of each sticker was information about the planet. You could peel that part off and save it when you were ready to use the sticker.

"Let's go into the closet," said Rosalie, "and stick the planets on the wall. We'll watch them glow."

"Later," said Max. "There's something I have to do first."

"What?" asked Rosalie.

"You know that box of Weird-O's you were talking about? I just want to check out that cute little Moon Walker. Only fifty cents and one proof of purchase."

"Oh, no," said Rosalie, rolling her eyes upward. "Here we go again."

"Why not?" asked Max. "Who knows? Maybe someday I'll be an astronaut."

Here's a list of all the
Redfeather Books from Henry Holt

Cory Coleman, Grade 2
by Larry Dane Brimner

The Fourth-Grade Four
by Marilyn Levinson

Max Malone and the Great Cereal Rip-off
by Charlotte Herman

Monstra Vs. Irving
by Stephen Manes

Snakes Are Nothing to Sneeze At
by Gabrielle Charbonnet

Something Special
by Emily Rodda

The 24-Hour Genie
by Lila Sprague McGinnis

Weird Wolf
by Margery Cuyler